MW01064686

Another Sommer-Time Story™

By Carl Sommer
Illustrated by Enrique Vignolo

Permissions
Advance Publishing, Inc.
6950 Fulton St.
Houston, TX 77022

www.advancepublishing.com

First Edition
Printed in Malaysia

Library of Congress Cataloging-in-Publication Data

Sommer, Carl, 1930-
Spike the rebel / by Carl Sommer ; illustrated by Enrique Vignolo. -- 1st ed.
p. cm. -- (Another Sommer-time story)
Summary: Spike enjoys being rebellious and rude, bullying and tattling on his classmates, and generally being mean, but after he falls into one of his own traps and hurts himself, his life is transformed. Includes a worksheet and a pledge about good behavior.
ISBN-10: 1-57537-072-7 (library binding : alk. paper)
ISBN-10: 1-57537-023-9 (hardcover : alk. paper)
ISBN-13: 978-1-57537-072-9 (library binding : alk. paper)
ISBN-13: 978-1-57537-023-1 (hardcover : alk. paper) [1. Behavior--Fiction. 2. Conduct of life--Fiction. 3. Bullies--Fiction.] I. Vignolo, Enrique, 1961- ill. II. Title.

PZ7.S696235Spi 2007
[E]--dc22

2006027519

Another Sommer-Time Story™

Debbie politely introduced herself to the boy next door when she moved into the neighborhood. "My name is Debbie. What's yours?"

Spike, whose real name was Philip, stuck out his chest and growled, "I'm Spike the rebel, the troublemaker!"

"Okay," whispered Debbie as she rode away on her bike.

Spike was mean. All the kids were afraid of him, except Mary. She had an older brother who would protect her. After chasing a group of kids, Spike said to Mary, “I love to get kids into trouble.”

Mary pointed her finger in Spike’s face and said, “You’re mean!”

“The only one I care about is myself!” Spike snapped back.

“You’d better watch out,” warned Mary. “One day you’ll get into big trouble acting like that.”

Spike rode away laughing and saying, “Not *me*! I can *always* take care of myself.”

Spike's parents loved him. But whenever they tried to teach him how to behave, he got mad. Spike *always* wanted to do things *his* way.

He never made his bed or put his toys and clothes away. He refused to do any work around the house. His parents constantly had to correct

him for his bad manners:

Don't reach across the table.
Say "Please" if you want something.
Eat with your fork, not with your fingers.
Chew with your mouth closed.
Cover your mouth when you cough.
Say "Thank you" when you receive a gift.

Spike never wanted to get his hair cut; he felt his long hair made him look tough and mean. When anyone asked him his name, he crossed his arms and growled, "I'm Spike the rebel, the troublemaker!"

The only one Spike cared about was himself. When he rode the school bus, he loved to tease the

girls in front of him. He poked them and pulled their hair. When younger kids passed by him, he often stuck out his foot to trip them. When they fell, he laughed saying, “Don’t be so clumsy! Don’t you know how to walk?”

Often the bus driver had to report him for his bad behavior.

Spike was a tattletaler. It was not that he wanted to help his teacher or class; he wanted to see other kids get into trouble.

When classmates did something wrong,

Spike would shoot up his hand and yell, "Teacher!"

Then Spike would gleefully tell the teacher what had happened.

One day during playtime Spike stuck out his foot as a boy ran past him. The boy fell and hit his chin on the curb. Spike laughed and said, "Don't you know how to run?"

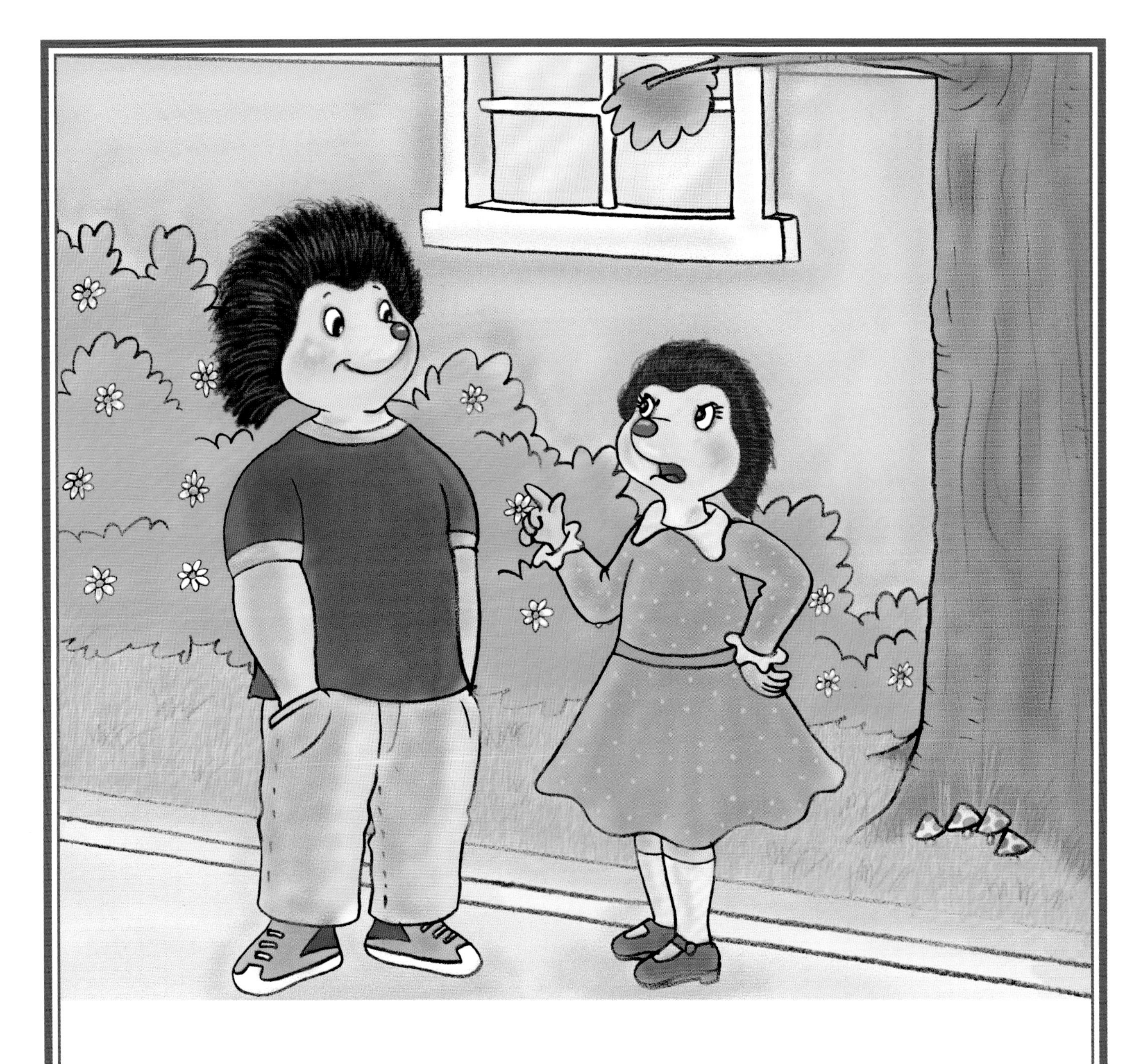

When Mary saw what Spike had done, she looked him in the eye and asked, "Why are you so mean? I saw you trip him!"

"I didn't trip him," snapped Spike. "He doesn't know how to run."

"Yes, you did!" insisted Mary. "I warn you. One day all the mean things you've done will come back to haunt you."

"That's what *you* think," sneered Spike. He stuck out his chest and boasted, "I'm not afraid of *anything*!"

Summertime came and Spike's family packed their van to go camping. When it was time to unload the van and put up the tent, Spike disappeared into the woods. Spike hated to do any kind of work.

After making sure the van was unloaded and the tent was up, Spike appeared with a few twigs for the fire.

"Where have you been?" asked Dad.

"I've been searching for firewood," he explained.

"Spike," said Dad, "there's firewood everywhere. You didn't have to spend that much time searching."

"Yes, I did," insisted Spike. "It was hard finding wood where I looked."

When Spike saw a boy at a nearby campsite with a BB gun, he became excited. He walked over and asked, “Can I shoot the BB gun?”

“Sure,” said Billy.

“Can we shoot the BB gun right now?” asked Spike.

“Let’s go.”

Off they went into the woods.

Billy took an empty can and placed it on a rock. “Let’s see who can hit the can the most,” said Billy.

Billy handed the BB gun to Spike so he could go first. They shot the BB gun a few times. Then Spike saw a bird in the tree. He quickly turned around and shot at the bird. But he missed.

“Don’t shoot at birds!” yelled Billy.

“What are you complaining about?” asked Spike. “I didn’t hit the bird.”

The next day Spike took a walk through the woods. When he saw a canoe, he looked to see if anyone was around. “Good!” he exclaimed. “I’m taking this canoe for a ride.”

Spike pushed the canoe into the water and began paddling.

After paddling a short distance, he saw an eagle fly into a nest. “Ohhhh!” he exclaimed. “I wish I had that BB gun. I could get myself an eagle feather.”

As Spike paddled down the river, he saw a cable with a sign warning him not to go any farther.

"The river can't be that bad," thought Spike. "I'm strong. I certainly can paddle this little canoe back. I'll just go a short distance."

Spike lifted the cable and coasted down the river. Then he saw another sign, "STOP! Dangerous Waterfall!"

"I can also handle this," he boasted.

The river became narrower, and the canoe went faster and faster. "This is fun!" he yelled.

Then Spike heard a strange sound. “That must be the waterfall,” he said. “I’d better start paddling back.”

He turned the canoe around and began paddling back. He paddled back as hard as he could, but the canoe kept going towards the waterfall. Suddenly he realized he was in deep trouble. He screamed as loud as he could, “Help!!!! Help!!!! I’m going over the waterfall!”

With the noise of the waterfall, no one could hear him. “I can’t do anything!” he screamed.

He flung himself to the bottom of the canoe and put his hands over his head. Spike and the canoe went flying over the waterfall. The canoe smashed against the rocks, but Spike was thrown into the air and landed in deep water.

As Spike sank deep into the water, he thought for sure he was going to drown. He struggled desperately for air. “I can’t hold my breath much longer,” he cried. Suddenly he popped up to the surface.

“I’m alive!” he shouted. “I’m alive!” He quickly swam to shore.

As Spike walked back to the campsite, he boasted, “Nothing can stop me! I went over the waterfall and nothing happened. I’m not afraid of anything!”

When he came to the campsite, his mother asked, "Where have you been? We've been looking everywhere for you. And why are you so wet?"

"I was playing by the lake," lied Spike, "and I fell into the water."

The next day Spike saw Billy and his family leave to go on a long hike. He snuck into their tent and found Billy's BB gun in a duffle bag. "Now I can get myself an eagle feather," he said.

Spike picked up the gun and walked to the eagle's nest and waited. "I see the eagle!" he exclaimed.

When the eagle flew close, he carefully aimed the BB gun and pulled the trigger. "Bang!"

The eagle gave a loud screech and fell into the lake. "Oh good!" he exclaimed. "I got him!"

When Spike saw two eagle feathers float towards him, he shouted, "Am I ever lucky! I even got two eagle feathers!"

The next day a notice came from the park ranger stating that an eagle was shot with a BB gun. The report asked, “Does anyone know of someone with a BB gun?”

When Spike heard that the park ranger was looking for a BB gun, he waited until no one was at Billy’s campsite. Then he placed one of the eagle feathers with Billy’s BB gun inside the duffle bag.

Spike went to his dad and said, “The family at the next campsite has a BB gun.”

“We need to tell the park ranger,” said Spike’s dad.

“I’ve seen Billy shoot at birds,” lied Spike. “He probably shot that eagle.”

When the park ranger came to Billy's campsite, he said, "I heard you have a BB gun. May I see it?"

"Sure," said Billy as he went to get the duffle bag.

When the ranger looked inside the duffle bag, he noticed an eagle feather. "Where did you get this eagle feather?"

"I don't know," said Billy.

The ranger took out the feather and said, "This is a fresh eagle feather, and we have a dead eagle killed by a BB gun."

“We weren’t here yesterday,” said Billy. “Besides, I never shoot at birds. Someone must have borrowed my BB gun.”

“Then you should take better care of your BB gun,” replied the ranger. “I’m going to press charges against you because of the dead eagle.”

“We can prove we weren’t here yesterday,” said Billy’s dad. “And I know my son always tells the truth.”

“I’m sorry,” said the ranger, “but the evidence points that you did it.”

When Spike came home from camping, he became even meaner. He thought by being tough and mean it would make him happy. But it did not.

One of his tricks was to set traps on the park bike trails. One day he dug a hole and covered it with cardboard, dirt, and leaves. Then he hid behind a tree to see if someone would fall.

Debbie happened to be riding down the bike trail. She hit the hole, tumbled over the handle bars, and hit her head hard on the ground. Spike came out from behind the tree laughing and saying, "Don't you know how to ride your bike, Debbie?"

Debbie held her head and cried as Spike rode off laughing.

Spike set many traps along the bike trails. One day as he was riding his bike, he said, "I'll ride down one more trail, and then I'll go home."

As he raced down the hill, he hit a rock that he had covered with leaves. As he went flying through the air his leg hit a broken branch. When he hit the ground, he heard a bone snap in his leg.

“Ouchhhh!!!!” he screamed.

When he looked at his leg, he cried, “My leg is broken, and I can’t get up!”

Then he yelled as loud as he could, “Help me! Somebody help me!”

No one heard him. Spike became frightened. He kept screaming as loud as he could, but still no one heard him. He became weaker and weaker.

Debbie and Mary happened to be riding home on their bikes when they heard a faint sound coming from the woods. “Stop!” said Mary. “I think I hear someone.”

They stood and listened. “It’s someone yelling for help,” said Debbie.

Mary frowned and sighed, “I know who that is. That’s Spike. I can always tell his mean voice.”

“We’ve got to help him,” insisted Debbie.

Mary sneered and said, “I wouldn’t help that guy. He’s a cruel big bully! Besides, you know how he laughed at you when you fell and got hurt.”

“I know he’s a cruel big bully,” argued Debbie, “but we’ve got to help him. He sounds like he’s really hurt and in deep trouble.”

Spike, weak from bleeding and the pain from his broken leg, began to think of all the mean things he did to others. Now that he was badly hurt, he desperately needed someone to help him. With tears flowing down his cheeks, he said with a choked voice, “I’ll never be mean again. I’m making everything right.”

Then Spike yelled as loud as he could, "Please! Somebody help me!" This was the first time Spike said on his own the word, "Please."

Meanwhile, Debbie raced home. She burst through the door and exclaimed, "Mom, I hear someone in the park screaming for help. I think it's Spike."

Debbie and her mother rushed to the park. Spike, his voice becoming weaker and weaker, continued to cry out, “Please! Somebody help me!”

“I’m coming,” shouted Debbie as she ran towards Spike. “It’s me, Debbie.”

“Oh no!” groaned Spike. “I’ve been so mean to her. When she sees me, she’ll turn around and leave, just like I did to her.”

Spike cried out and begged, “Please, Debbie, come and help me!”

When Debbie saw Spike, she ran to him and said, “My mother is coming to help you.”

“Thank you for coming,” whispered Spike as tears flowed down his cheeks. “I’m so sorry for being so mean to you. Please forgive me.”

“I forgive you,” said Debbie as she patted his head.

When Debbie’s mother came, she saw the deep gash on Spike’s leg. She quickly took out her cell phone and called for help.

Quickly the paramedics came. They put Spike on a stretcher and rushed him to the hospital.

As Spike lay on his bed, he heard the doctor say to his dad and mom, “If it weren’t for Debbie, Spike might have died.”

Spike shook all over when he heard what the doctor had said.

The next day when Debbie and her mother came to visit him, Spike said, “Thank you, Debbie for saving my life. Never again will I be mean. I’m going to be just like you and help others. To show that I’ve changed, please, don’t call me Spike anymore; just call me Philip.”

When Philip came out of the hospital he immediately got a haircut. When his leg got better, he said to himself, “I’m filling every trap I’ve ever made. And if I see any stones or branches on bike trails that are unsafe, even though I didn’t put them there, I’ll remove them also.”

He and Debbie began helping poor kids in the neighborhood. One day Philip said to Debbie, “I thought being tough and mean would make me happy, but I’ve discovered I’m much, much happier having friends and helping others.”

Spike or Philip Test

Are you like Spike or Philip?

Spike

___I don't say "Thank you" when I get a gift.

___I don't cover my mouth when I cough.

___I don't have table manners.

___I avoid doing chores in my home.

___I don't listen to my teachers.

___I don't obey school rules.

___I am a tattletaler.

___I am a bully.

___I am not kind to others.

___I never say "I'm sorry" when I do wrong.

___I don't respect the elderly.

___I tell lies.

___I don't obey my dad and mom.

Philip

___I say "Thank you" when I get a gift.

___I cover my mouth when I cough.

___I have table manners.

___I do my chores in my home.

___I listen to my teachers.

___I obey school rules.

___I am not a tattletaler.

___I am not a bully.

___I am kind to others.

___I quickly say "I'm sorry" when I do wrong.

___I respect the elderly.

___I tell the truth.

___I obey my dad and mom.

Here are some other words Philip began to say. "Excuse me," "pardon me," "you're welcome," "and please."

These are some compliments Philip gave to others. "Very good," "excellent," "awesome," "you're great," "terrific," "great job," and "keep up the good work."

I ______________________________ pledge that starting
Name

from today ______________________ I will do my best to
Date

become like Philip.